The Complete Tales of Lucy Gold

THE COMPLETE TALES OF LUCY GOLD

By
KATE BERNHEIMER

FC2
TUSCALOOSA

Published by FC2, an imprint of The University of Alabama Press,
with support provided by the Publishing Program at the University of
Houston–Victoria.

Address all editorial inquiries to: Fiction Collective Two, University of
Houston–Victoria, School of Arts and Sciences, Victoria, TX 77901-5731

Cover and book design: Lou Robinson
Typefaces: Janson and Commerce
Produced and printed in the United States of America
∞
The paper on which this book is printed meets the minimum requirements of
American National Standard for Information Sciences—Permanence of Paper
for Printed Library Materials, ANSI Z39.48–1984

Library of Congress Cataloging-in-Publication Data

Bernheimer, Kate.
    The complete tales of Lucy Gold / by Kate Bernheimer. —1st ed.
        p. cm.
    ISBN 978-1-57366-159-1 (pbk. : alk. paper) —ISBN 978-1-57366-821-7
(electronic)
1. Young women—Fiction. 2. Women animators—Fiction. 3. Magic—
Fiction. I. Title.
PS3602.E76C662 2011
813'.6—dc22
                                        2010017784

The author wishes to acknowledge the German, Russian, and Yiddish fairy tales on which portions of this novel are based:

From Chinese Fairy Tales and Fantasies, "Test of Conviction"

From Grimms' Tales for Young and Old, "The Golden Key," "The Star Travelers," "Clever Else," "Two Families," "Friendly Animals (I & II)" "The Messengers of Death," "The Death of The Hen," "The Three Spinners," "A Riding Tale"

From Russian, "The Goat Comes Back," "Anecdote," "Beasts in a Pit"

From Yiddish, "Things Can Always Get Worse," "Clever Kashinke and Foolish Bashinke," "The Bright Sun Will Bring it to Light"

The author also wishes to acknowledge the fairy tales reproduced here by permission of the publisher in their complete translated form. They are listed in the order in which they appear in the novel.
"Friendly Animals I & II" © Anchor Books
"Anecdote" © Pantheon Books
"The Golden Key" © Anchor Books

But the "consolation" of fairy tales has another aspect than the imaginative satisfaction of ancient desires. Far more important is the consolation of the Happy Ending. Almost I would venture to assert that all complete fairy-stories must have it. At least I would say that Tragedy is the true form of Drama, its highest function; but the opposite is true of Fairy-story. Since we do not appear to possess a word that expresses this opposite—I will call it *Eucatastrophe*.

—J. R. R. Tolkien

For Merry and Ketzia

chapter one

THE GOLDEN KEY

One winter day, when the ground outside my cottage was covered in snow, I went into the forest to bring back some wood. I loaded the wood onto a sled. I was so cold, I thought I would make a fire and sit beside it a while before I went home. No one waited for me in the cottage, apart from the dear spiders and mice. I cleared a space in the snow by scraping at it with a stick, intending to sit down and warm my bones. Soon I uncovered a golden key. "Where there's a key," I thought, "there is surely some magic." You might expect that I desired to dig more, and discover a locked iron box. You might expect me to have wished that this iron box were full of glittering things. You might expect me to have fit the key perfectly into the lock of the box, and that I would have turned it and turned it with hope. You might even wonder what terrible marvels I found in there, what sadness or evil they brought into the world. Yet I had no such desire to discover the sadness or evil. Sure as the forest is made up of trees and dirt and needles and worms, these are now and can always be lucky trees and dirt and needles and worms. It's a trick of the mind, this desire for peace. Yet just the same, I can assure you no story has ever waited for me. Only the darkened night with death by three. All happiness once was taken from me. Please solve the riddle; I can no longer speak.

chapter two

Under the bed, in a worn cardboard shoebox, lies a stuffed monkey with a pink and smudged face, and a pink satin ribbon taped onto one ear. The monkey wears a pink plastic helmet and used to hang from the ceiling tied to a rope. Lucy Gold, the youngest of the four children, got the monkey from Ketzia, who got it from Merry. The monkey skipped over the brother, as it was pink. (He preferred rose, he always said.)

Lucy abides by favorite things—especially colors. Once, she overheard an angular woman announce to Mrs Gold in the kitchen, "I disdain whimsy," and wondered how anyone could. Lucy prefers whimsy to anything else—except perhaps Monkee, with her almost-gone fur and fraying rope—or was it a noose, as Merry once said? Lucy rejects the creepiness of the noose-notion, and concentrates rapt attention on the goodly essence of the poignant, sad monkey.

Though very young, Lucy has already learned quite a bit about the world that she lives in, the attention that it desires: about her two older sisters who don't get along and about how to get along with both of them well. She sees that the straight-haired one who cries is annoying to the curly-haired one who is mean; and she sees that to avoid annoying the mean one, she must exude charm. To avoid hurting the sad one, she must comfort her lavishly in private.

Lucy has learned that her brother does not have much to do with the sisters, including herself, though he does not seem to have much to do with anything at all except maybe his blocks. He does like having his fingernails painted by Grandma—and who doesn't, with that lamp in the shape of a hand that you rest your own hand upon during the painting? (Glows yellow, gets warm.)

The only naturally sunny child of all the Gold girls, Lucy cherishes the airy nursery room in which she sleeps, with its orange gauze curtains and the heater's radiant hiss. Ketzia and Merry sleep in two newer rooms down the hall: Ketzia's pink, containing a dollhouse, Merry's green and featuring a toadstool lamp. The brother's room is blue. Mysteriously it glows with video games. In summer, a box set in Lucy's windowsill roars. Each night, whether winter or summer, autumn or spring, Lucy lies perfectly still in her sleep: stunning expression upon her face, hands clasped under her chin. On the pink sheets are depicted green fairies, half moons and violet stars.

Here in gilded frame the glorious childhood world: four little children, moving through rooms as through a series of books. Miniature, the tiny, dead-end perfection. Intuitive from the beginning, Lucy softly, easily dreams.

And yet, there is nothing more tedious than hearing about someone's dreams. Consider instead these provocative questions: *What is the relationship between the fairies and Lucy? Is it they who breathe life into her, or she who is ascendant for them?*

chapter three

PENNIES, NICKELS, AND DIMES

I'm going to tell you something, so listen. Long ago I learned to be happy. I was happy for all of my days.

I had the birds, who told me the weather, and I had my rooms. When I first moved to the forest, I had denounced everything else. So I often sat at the window listening to the birds and the wind and the snow falling down from the sky. That is all I desired.

Sometimes, a human person would pass by my hut and stare curiously at me through the fogged windows. I would wave him away—gently, of course. I waved "Go away" with no malice, no nerves. A sort of woodland *Go-Away* trill, if you can imagine.

I had long ago left my parents' house and all childhood trinkets behind—a giant trombone, glittering paints, all of my toe shoes and tutus. I was too blissed out to bring them along. I was that airy-fairy.

I arranged to be awake and asleep according to nature—that beautiful beast, that loveliest monster—each given day. I rose with the sun, and when the sun was finished for evening, my own day was finished too.

There was no need for news from the city. News is

not usually good, so why seek it? During my lifetime the news has always been bad. May it reasonably request to be called the "news?" I think not. (True news is worth listening for, and more radiant or awful. Anyone can hear it, if she only tries.)

Instead, I spent my days walking the forest dressed appropriately for the weather, whatever it was. When it was summer, I wore little, and when it was winter, I bundled up. It is not that I cared for myself, nor whether I lived or died. I loved life—yes—but not my own personal possession of it in my humble container. Besides, any reasonable person who has the means will dress for the weather. It would only be spiteful to do anything else.

In spring I looked for nests, particularly those of the robins. Robins sometimes nest twice in a season. Isn't that a wonderful fact? Certain facts provide such simple pleasure. I allowed myself the happiness of observing the robins' double-nesting season. Oh the robins—their little red bellies, those dignified coats.

I kept myself occupied thus.

I had no need for money. I had all the wood that one would require for fire, and when the robins' nests sometimes would fail, and fall to the ground, and the robins depart for elsewhere, I had fine little blue eggs for supper. If they'd fallen down freshly, there was no need even to cook them—thus no need to waste any wood on a fire, if I wasn't cold. (Mind you, if the robins did linger, I would do what I could to place the nest back in a tree. Yet I found that more often the failed nests were abandoned, after a few long moments of robin-grieving. And how I grieved with them.) Dearest robins, my precious friends!

Did you ever love something so much you just wanted to eat it?

I was so poor that I slept on a bed made of hay. I had gathered the hay from the barn. When I first was sent to the forest, I came upon the cottage as in a dream, and I went out to the barn and saw what there was to see: a ladder, a bucket, an old dying mare.

I went to the well and filled up the bucket, but the mare did not want the water. What could I do? I gave her my blessing and left her there in a halo of flowers. Gathering hay in my arms, I went into the cottage and made a small mattress. I had nothing to call my own except for the clothes I wore on my back and a few small objects (matchbook, storybook, lantern) and now the thatched cottage and the barn and apparently an old dying mare and some hay and some water.

Lovingly, I cared for the mare every day. There was little for us to do in the woods but keep company there. Sometimes I worked on the clearing, making space for foxgloves and fiddlehead ferns. It is strange, but the fields did not speak to me nor did the flowers! Not even the mare. Before I had been banished, or stolen, I could hear ladybugs talking—dust motes whispering—flowerheads expanding their lungs.

Still, I had my kindness. If a child came along, walking down the dirt road to the clearing, I would feed her some morsels.

And if a child walked down the dirt road wearing nothing, I would give her a burlap sack for her back. I would say, "Here, put this on."

And if a child approached me and told me he was cold—why of course, I would bring him nearer the fire. But not too near!

Happy is as happy does.

And Lucy is my Name-O.

Of course, none of this ever happened. I lived deep in the forest. No child ever did come.

Once, it is true, I found my *own* self in need of food. I walked down the dirt road to another road and from there, on pavement into the town. I passed the post office, and the postmistress peered out a window. I passed the town hall, and saw a meeting room there all full of men; one hit a gavel upon a table. It seemed the gavel just floated in air a long time before it hit down, very silent. I passed by three churches, their windows closed tight. I passed by a lake, and then I reached the town dump.

Yet once there I had no sense of what to do—the bins were all tightly locked. Even the bears, so great and needful, could not have gotten in them. But there were no bears. They all were gone.

So I turned and walked home. I went hungry until something grew in the ground. That's the whole story: once I was hungry and I walked and I walked, and then I went home to my dying mare.

Obladi oblada life goes on on la la la la life goes on, I sang in her ear.

Whether I ought to have gone on looking for pennies, nickels, or dimes in that pine-needled forest, I don't think so. One should look skyward for stars and leave them home in the heavens. And, looking down, seek the snails in their shells, some of earth's most wonderful gifts to us humans. Those humble residences! Don't dare step on them.

In that forest I found a new and peaceable home. It was different from any I ever had known. It was a new kind of happiness—I kept my ear cocked to the clearing, waiting for someone to come take me home. I was happy when I thought of my mother.

And so I called the old dying mare Mama. Mama! I would say to her. How I love you! Oh my mama my mama my love!

About that, we laughed and we laughed. It was too bad, but we laughed so hard that the mare up and died.

But she died happy, I tell you. And so did I.

B y the age of four, Lucy had denounced birthday parties, peacefully intuiting them to be selfish events—
she asked instead to celebrate her parents and sisters and
brother on June 1 every year.

At the age of five she wrote a letter to Mr and Mrs
Gold. It read, "Thank you for your cooperation. No GIFTS
OR CONTRIBUTIONS." The phrases had been painstakingly
copied (it took several hours) from a letter she found on
Mrs Gold's desk from the Temple, inviting her to either
a meeting, a funeral, or a bat mitzvah. (Mr Gold was an
atheist, while Mrs Gold had tentative leanings; in later
years, this reversed for reasons that still are not known.)

In addition to finding the garish festivities of birthday parties a sort of *moral* embarrassment, Lucy believed
she had already gathered enough gifts of consequence
in her life—she felt no need for further attachments to
toys; those she had were so beloved and spectacular, so
shamefully in excess already. In a metal trunk at the foot
of her bed—the very same trunk Mrs Gold had taken to
camp when she was young, which either was or was not a
camp where you might have been killed—Lucy kept her

favorite belongings. This trunk that resembled the treasure chest of a pirate, and also evoked danger: Lucy did not want to add to its collection.

Among the items in there: a sewing kit, a plastic doll, a knitted skirt. The sewing kit and plastic doll had been Merry's first and then Ketzia's, and were rather broken. The sewing kit held needles and thread all tangled in a glinting mess. This treacherous bundle was itself rolled up inside the knitted skirt, which Grandma had made. (Yellow, pom-poms, and fringe.) The doll, naked and dirty, had eyelids but under, no eyes; by the time she'd been passed down to Lucy, they'd either fallen out or been removed, possibly during a game her sisters played called The Punish, a game about which they both spoke with great fervor and pride.

The missing eyes of the doll did bother Lucy, so for her ninth birthday she reluctantly and with feelings of guilt did ask for a present: that the doll-eyes be fixed. Mrs Gold took the pretty, unnamed, and blind creature to the Doll Hospital in the town center. With Lucy at her elbow, she had, by telephone, arranged for an operation. The delivery and operation took place while Lucy was at school, but the Doll Hospital was very real; this was not just a story. Everyone in town knew about the Doll Hospital. It had brought the town very great fame at one time.

But the Doll Hospital botched the procedure (so rare of those well-trained and fine dolly doctors! so unexpected!): the doll stared malevolently, not sweetly, somehow, when it returned home, by mail in a carton.

Oh, our dear and resourceful Lucy! Ever the optimist here.

Using her magic, Lucy pronounced the doll dead. Then the sewing kit simply came in handy to sew the lids down. The poncho came in handy to wrap the doll corpse; and the pirate's chest came in handy as the doll's coffin. *Came in handy*, thought Lucy with a shudder—what a terrible phrase. (Perhaps just the word *handy* was wrong.)

Thus, on the eve of June 1, after no birthday cake—for none was requested—and no birthday song—Lucy lay in bed in a pink flannel nightgown, rubbing the cold soles of her feet together beneath the pink coverlet. A slight breeze blew the orange gauze curtains ajar, letting some moonlight into the room. In the pink-orange haze of her mind, Lucy thought of the doll.

And *Lucy Lucy Lucy* she heard—the sound of a breeze sliding in through the window, scented with lilac. Her little body gave a small, floral shudder. From then on she was enchanted, you see.

chapter five

THINGS CAN ALWAYS GET WORSE

Once upon a time, a dark force took my spirit away and replaced it with nothing.

This happened when I was employed by Magic Movies, and soon after I was no longer employed and became impoverished in material ways.

Too grateful for a happy childhood to ask my parents for money, I stood in line to receive free supper downtown. (At the time I didn't realize that one could rummage for berries on bushes or bake bread out of dirt. And now I understand that fairies choose to live simply on air.)

One day—I am not proud to report this—weak and befuddled by hunger, I complained to the sky. Raising my fist high I denounced not only humans, who deserve it of course, but also the entire planet itself.

And for good reason, as soon as I raised my fist and proclaimed my frustration—a hump just like my grandmother's grew on my back! And then on top of the hump, a small donkey grew, and on top of the donkey, a bird.

"Oh, dear," I thought.

I was a little bit worried, but more for the animals than

for myself. I had no way to feed two mouths in addition to mine. How would I care for these darling creatures? No matter the hump. I rather liked the lift it gave to my soul.

And, I considered, it was true that until then I had suffered from loneliness, for I was the only happy person I knew. Now I could imagine I might become slightly less happy too! Perhaps this was a blessing and I would better fit in with a malcontent culture.

But no! After a few moments of such lunatic thinking, I was happy again and only worried for the donkey and bird.

After that, any time I did find a piece of bread or apple to eat, the donkey and the bird would snap their mouths at the bread or apple and take it from me, the donkey with her sweet glittering eyes, the bird with her pretty beak. What choice did I have as a good soul but to feed them?

The bird was easy to carry, but the donkey was heavy. All day long she would sort of lean her head forward upon my shoulder and turn her head, and stare into my eyes with great adoration.

"I really care about you," I told her. "I really like you a lot."

But it was only a matter of days before I was bent over with pain—just like my grandmother with her hump only worse—and it was then that I understood how we are all animals, dying each moment. Death, the eternal donkey of life, I thought.

This phrase filled me with such a light feeling that the donkey-skin and bird-feathers upon me (not to mention the lives they contained) became too heavy to bear in the moment. Under their weight, I collapsed.

And I remember falling with a bright grin upon my face—"how lucky I am to have such fine companions!" was the thought that then entered my mind.

When I awoke I was in a very white room on a very white bed and seven men in white coats peered down at my face. In the corner of the room I saw in a heap a vast number of colorful feathers (a pink one wafted up in the ventilation). Over my body was a donkey-skin blanket. Into my arm dripped some kind of potion—apple-scented and pink. A new sort of smile seemed lodged on my face.

Oh, the indignity of this!

The terrible bliss I felt then—I never had known it before! It was catastrophic. It was unreal. Where was my friend the donkey? Where was my friend the bird? And flat, flat, I tell you. Like my mood, my back was straight as a board.

I don't want the fake magic? I said to the doctors. *I'm already happy?*

Never any reply.

After that, I became a new person.

After several courses of treatment, at last I was offered three choices. I pointed carefully to Door Number Three. Slowly it opened, onto the forest, straight from the hospital bed.

It took many months to clean the apple-pink meds from my veins, but eventually, I returned to my more natural condition. It was slightly more strange, slightly more distant, but I survived in the end. Well, for a while.

"Like This"

chapter six

O f the four Gold children, Lucy was the most beautiful—and the easiest of the three sisters to like. She
was never angry or sad. One could describe her as airy.
When the children would play together on rainy Sat-
urdays—indoor bowling, paint-by-the-numbers, oven-
baked glass—Lucy would watch with a joyous expression
as Merry bossed and Ketzia wept. It was not that she
thought this was how to behave, just that nothing else
ever occurred. She would watch with a rapt expression
any scene that took place. Lucy was light! (The brother
never featured in these childhood scenes; he would be off
by himself with his Erector Set, Legos, or trains.)

Good-natured as she was, every year Lucy anticipated
the first day of Passover more than any other day of the
year, and this year was no different from most. Around
the dining room table the four children sat and dutifully
waited for their turn to ask one of Four Questions. On
the Seder plate, an egg lolled next to a gnawed chicken
bone masquerading as that of a lamb. Parsley had been
chopped and put in a bowl together with salt water and
egg. And under a white cloth, the flat bread waited to be

hidden and found.

"Isn't it magical," Lucy gushed, and gazed at her father with adoration.

The Four Questions would beautifully be asked in order. But they weren't really questions! *Mah nishtanah.* They seemed to be pleas to a mother. This night is different from all other nights. This night is different.

Above the dinner table a garish portrait of a witch hung and cackled. The witch, with her green face and giant nose, frightened the Gold children though none would admit it, especially not Lucy. Lucy believed fear could not be proven, after all, to exist. Thus fear of an imaginative portrait would itself be insane.

Waiting her turn to say *mah, mah, mah nishtanah,* Lucy gnawed on the shank bone, swiped from the plate. She thought about the storybook waiting upstairs to be studied in bed. In this book, a witch grabbed at the hand of a boy, but the hand was really a bone. Now that was glorious sorcery, that story! And another, where a boy entered a room full of corpses that laughed! Now that gave her shivers!

The Spring has come, Mrs Gold read, *the song of the turtle is heard through the land.* The song of the turtle . . . Lucy sang in her mind . . . *gaaaaaaaaw mwaaaaaaaahhhhh. The fig tree giveth forth her figs,* Mrs Gold calmly continued. *When we were slaves in Egypt . . . toads . . . locusts . . . a plague* . . . the song of the turtle, Lucy thought. The song of the turtle. The song of the turtle sings out through the land.

chapter seven

GOOD LUCY

I was considered good-tempered when young, and my parents appreciated this in a house full of irrational children. My oldest sister was mean; my next-oldest was sad; and my brother was, you might say, slow to develop. It was left to me to be inoffensive—easily done as I considered life to be simply enchanting.

When I was seventeen, I decided to marry someone. It was not considered normal to get married so young, in that modern time. Perhaps it was my one moment of rebellion—a desire for early, good marriage!

My parents never said that they hoped for us girls to marry so young, as they themselves had very well done. In fact, it was something I knew might not please them. Yet what else was there for a happy girl to do but get married, I wondered. (My older sisters had different ideas about the tradition of marriage: Ketzia feared it, and Merry despised it of course.) It's not so much that I longed for or loved the idea; I just had a kindly relationship to it, as I did to everything possible under the sun.

One night, I invited a neighbor over for dinner—his name was Sam Han. I had been in love with him since third grade.

My mother put Chinese take-out—dumplings, egg rolls, and rice—onto the table and my father announced, "She's a true Jewish princess, this one. Wants Chinese every weekend."

"So airy she sees the wind coming. Such a fairy she hears the flies coughing," my mother addended.

"None of what they said about me is true," I confided to Sam.

This was a lie: I could hear the flies coughing, the wind coming; as for the moniker of Jewish princess, I found it quite pleasing! And I always have adored the Chinese.

Sam nodded his head. "I know, Lucy," he said, and he took my hand under the table. "If you really cared, you wouldn't be in the Blue Classroom at school." My school was public and progressive and didn't believe in calling some children gifted, advanced, or honored. Instead we were put into classrooms of colors—pink, violet, blue; and blue was the lowest achieving. Sam was in pink and it was rumored that he knew the Latin names of all wildflowers native to our small suburb; the precise distance between the earth and the moon; and the poetry of Sylvia Plath.

It is not true that I wasn't smart, but I didn't feel a need to prove my intelligence to anyone; either it would shine or would not shine to them, no matter as I knew that the light that shone upon us all was divine and was wondrous. Unlike my older sister Merry, who was very smart but so mean she could only do math and not reading, and unlike Ketzia, who felt so sorry for herself she couldn't think about numbers and only could think about books, I was good, my mind free and untarnished. I was a child in the light of the world.

The truth is, I didn't bother to try or not to try at my schooling. I could not understand the convention of proving I had or had not mastered certain inventions, however interesting they could surely be proven to be, like math or like spelling. It is difficult to explain, but always there was something else that interested me ever so much more . . . something just out of reach, like heaven, horizon, or dream.

I murmured a thank you to Sam for understanding that I was not stupid or smart, but rather neutral—I mean, sort of abstract. I had the flatness of a grey stone in the hand of a spirit, I think. I mean this in a good way, as an essence of being.

Of course I allowed Sam Han to hold my hand as I walked him up the street to his house. He was not as small as his stooped-over father, but he did have to stand on the sidewalk to kiss me goodnight, while I stayed on the cobblestone street.

"Lucy Gold," he said, "I will never forget you. I've been meaning to tell you for a very long time that you are most important to me, and you always will be. You have been a loyal friend who has never questioned my interest in wildflowers, moon travel, or death."

Gazing up at the moon the whole way, I walked myself home and went up to my parents' room where they were in bed. My mother wore a flannel nightgown with a pattern of tulips and maidens on it. She was reading a fat book with gold letters stamped on the cover, and a red Swastika on the spine. My father was in his underwear and socks, newspaper in front of his face. This was such a beautiful and peaceful scene I did not want to interrupt; why deny them their few moments of privacy in an otherwise unselfish existence? Yet they heard me try to slip past without a word and rushed to the hallway.

"So?" my father said.

"So?" my mother said.

"I'd like to marry Sam Han," I said. "Then I could be Lucy Han, and convert to Chinese." In all my prettiest imaginings, this was the best one I ever had come up with, I thought.

My parents exchanged glances, but said nothing, and went back to bed. Curious, as they themselves had married at twenty. Also curious as they usually were riveted by my every delicate word.

I danced into the bedroom, kissed them both goodnight on the cheek, and rushed to my room in a blissful condition. Sam Han loved me, he loved me, he did! And I did so love Sam Han. His tippy-toed kiss had revealed endless affection and from his words I knew that he understood how I understood him.

I sat at the edge of my bed. I put my feet on the treasure trunk and kicked it. *Oh treasure chest, hope chest, my dearest friend,* I said. *Sam Han loves me.*

Oddly, the chest sounded hollow. I opened the trunk and brightness shot at me. For a moment I had no sight. When I'd regained my vision, I discovered all of my treasures were gone.

The next morning I learned that Sam Han had died, taken by his very own hand.

And I know this will shock you, for I was always so

happy, your airy fairy girl of the woods, the girl who lives in, but doesn't know, darkness: that is just how I died too in the end.

"A House Full of Irrational Children"

chapter eight

From a young age, Lucy liked to keep things tidy in boxes or shoes or in nutshells or pockets—like many children, she found it pleasant for things to fit into this or that place.

And so one object she particularly admired was neither a book nor a toy. Rather, it was a box with a spine like a book. Inside of the box resided one eensy doll. The doll had a cloth body with stuffing, and a china head. The spine of the box read *A Doll's Book*. When you opened the cover, you revealed plastic with three little crannies: one for the doll, one for some fabric, and one for the clothes that you made.

Merry had helped Lucy make things for the doll. She sewed a hot-pink sleeping bag you closed with a plastic pearl button. Ketzia also had helped by writing a poem for the doll to keep in the box, to keep her from getting lonely. "Oh China Doll," the poem began, "How I Long for Thee," and on from there. "You are my lonely doll/ You are my friend / I will love you / Until the end." Lucy found the poem wonderfully sentimental, and she obliged her sister. It was easy to so oblige her, knowing how her feelings were hurt often enough by the very act of living itself. Lucy folded the bit of paper on which the poem was typed and slipped it into the hot-pink sleeping bag along with the doll. A doll in satin inside a box! A doll in a book that wasn't even a book! Tiny things inside tiny things, so very appealing!

Yet with a boxed series of volumes about a Jewish family of girls, Lucy had a particularly conflicted relationship. On the one hand, she felt drawn to read again and again about their lost library books and the late fines for them, and about how their mother, to test their cleaning abilities, would hide pennies here and there inside the dust and see if the girls found all of the pennies while doing their chores. In one story, the youngest daughter sat on a pickle barrel and ate some crackers inside a store.

Lucy kept her books late from the library for a time in imitation, and requested that Mrs Gold hide pennies from her—but Mrs Gold didn't like the girls to help with the cleaning or to hoard money. Soon after these failures (late fines, no pennies, no chores) Lucy turned against this Jewish series. It would not do, Lucy recognized at a very young age, to try to live inside stories.

One had to love the world, already teeming with beautiful things.

And while, like her sisters, she did enjoy dolls—what child would not find fascination in a creature called Baby Alive—there was something unsettling to Lucy about them from time to time. Lugging a doll around a room, a doll that could "poo" or could "pee"—there was something troubling to this, like having a dead-seeming double or oddly beloved curse.

Often, Lucy found herself sitting at the edge of her bed, kicking her feet in the air. Picking tiny white balls off the chenille comforter, she'd stare at the shelf where her dolls and books sat. She would will herself not to play with them, especially *A Doll's Book*—without knowing quite why. Usually, she failed. And who could blame her?

Sometimes to distract herself from *A Doll's Book*, she struggled to find affection for the troll in a jar, labeled Doll Jam, which had appeared in a Christmas stocking. It seemed to be made out of a nylon stocking. Being Lucy, she managed to find warmth for the wrinkled jarred creature, though it did cause her unrest. Doll Jam disappeared sometime in her teens.

And to this very day, every so often Lucy tucks the dear China Doll into her sleeping bag where she sleeps in the forest. And every so often she takes her out, looks directly into her wide-open eyes, and ever-so-faintly smiles. Then she reads Ketzia's poem, still folded inside.

In the dark of the woods, it brings her some light.

chapter nine

A t Triple E, as the wooded farm became known when the sign EGGS, PERENNIALS, & ETCETERA was hit by lightning that toppled the P, I had a very good job. I had lived in the woods for several years without gainful employment, making my way with what I could find for free. However, as it turned out, even I who wished to rely on no one but the dirt and myself discovered that employment could prove very useful even if lacking in wonder.

Triple E had four kinds of chickens and I was responsible for gathering eggs every morning. They laid colored eggs: pink, brown, blue, and green. I was to arrange them in cartons and to distribute the colors evenly among the cartons. People with wealth belonged to the farm and would come pick up their eggs, and if they felt another family were receiving better eggs, more pinks, greens or blues, they would complain. "The Smith family carton has two pinks, and ours only has one." Whatever color was lacking in a family's carton they decided was magic— more than delicious, but golden somehow. (Thankfully I was not asked to interact with the customers.)

After gathering and sorting the eggs I deadheaded the

garden's voluminous flowers. Then I divided them, and kept them well fed. Yes, even flowers need to eat! Eggs and flowers took up the morning, and in the afternoon I focused on Etcetera.

Oh joy, I say with no passion.

Etcetera was carving dolls out of wood. When I inquired about Triple E's sign for Help Needed, I did not for a moment imagine or dream I would be making dolls, as I have always disdained them. A love of dolls is neurotic. But, as it turns out in one of those cruel twists of what others call fate (and I call "whatever"), I have a talent for carving dolls out of wood. This was discovered to my disappointment at the time of application. To be hired, I had to pass some small tests.

First, I had to clean out the chicken coop. This required me to tolerate odors. Second, I sprinkled flowerbeds with manure, shoveled out of the fields. This required me to tolerate odors. And third, I was handed a small piece of wood and a chisel. I was asked to make a doll with a kindly expression. This required me to tolerate something I still cannot name.

I found that I had quite a knack for finding sweet humor in wood. The farmers could not believe their good fortune when I passed all three of the examination components so easily. There were not, apparently, many who had the talent for both tolerating bad odors and for doll making. To me, it seems a natural if unfortunate pairing.

My speculation is that because I am balanced I can perceive imbalance in others, and thus correct it. Chickens are sensitive; so too are flowers. What is more surprising is my talent with wood, and for the making of dolls. Indeed! Dolls that children come from far and wide to purchase. I have not quite defined my position but each doll needs a human, or more likely it is the reverse: it is my job to correct an absence in children.

By now I have admitted an ability to suffer the feelings of wood.

And it is a great comfort to work in such a quiet place—here in the back of the cottage, in what used to be the apple room, before the apple trees got diseased, before the bees stopped coming to pollinate them. Thankfully, the farmers understand my request that the children not be allowed to peer through the windows at me.

It would be alarming for them to see me with their dolls, to see me using the knife on their faces. There are some things children never should see.

chapter ten

"FRIENDLY ANIMALS"

A little orphan girl sat spinning at the foot of the ramparts, when suddenly a grass snake crawled out of a crack in the wall. Quickly she spread out her blue kerchief beside her, the kind that snakes love to sit on. When the snake saw that, it turned around and vanished, but soon came back, carrying a tiny gold crown, put the crown on the kerchief, and went away.

The little girl picked up the glittering crown, which was made of finely spun gold. After a while the snake came a second time. When it saw that the crown wasn't there any more, it crept back to the wall. Stricken with grief, it beat its head against the stone as long as its strength held out, and finally lay there dead. If the little girl had left the crown lying on the kerchief, the snake would probably have brought her more treasures from its hole.

chapter eleven

Oh Christmas tree, oh Christmas tree, how are thy leaves so verdant, Lucy sang as she placed strands of tinsel one by one, one by one, on the branches. In the brown den with its brown curtains and beige rug, the green tree glowed in the corner, lit by the roaring fire Lucy's mother had built. Lucy lifted her rapt face to the top of the tree where Mrs Gold had perched not a star, but a dog—more precisely a photograph of a dachshund pasted on cardboard.

At Lucy's feet the family dog, Gretel, leapt and leapt and leapt and leapt at the tinsel. Laughing, Lucy continued to decorate the tree with the silver strands. Ketzia also was helping to decorate the tree, or so it seemed; for she had mysteriously held the same ornament, a glass angel with crown, in her hand for nearly an hour and had not hung it at all. Every now and then she would hold it up to a branch, begin to place the tiny metal loop there, and then shake her head and step back as if startled, only to stare at the tree again for a while. From time to time, Merry came in, crossed her arms on her chest, and either nodded or shook her head, and then left the room.

"How about hanging it here?" Lucy asked Ketzia, pointing to a bare branch at the front of the tree, which struck Lucy as a particularly choice spot for the angel.

Ketzia began to hang the angel there, and then withdrew her hand. She crept around to the back of the tree, which was entirely empty, facing the wall.

"I think maybe back here?" she said. "I think the tree is lonely back here."

Lucy watched as her sister hung the angel at last. Poor Ketzia! she thought. So . . . sensitive . . . so . . . weak. It wasn't normal to have to help your older sister fend for herself: that was supposed to be Ketzia's job, wasn't it, to help Lucy? And she knew never to ask Merry for anything. Thankfully, Lucy didn't need help. With her shiny brown hair and green eyes and her butterfly-grace, Lucy attracted only approval wherever she went—but she hardly noticed, as is the way of the pretty, not knowing what it was like to be looked at with pity for poor fortune in looks.

Lucy reached down and patted Gretel. Dear Gretel! Dear dog! Oh Gretel, she thought, kneeling down to hug her long body. Oh Gretel Gretel Gretel Gretel! *Oh Gretel dog oh Gretel dog, how I love thy fu-u-ur*, she sang, so happy, so glad. It was Christmas again!

chapter twelve

A dollmaker rarely is required to be inventive—at least the sort of dollmaker I am, who works with a paring knife and some wood. I do stray, from time to time, into apples—wizened faces to hang on string. Yet even the apples require no contribution from me. I simply read them.

In my old profession, I often had to learn new technology, and sometimes invent it; I was the Lead Figurist for a very famous studio, and built models for animation. All that dimension, all that 3-D expression! To be sure this was challenging work for a mind that prefers flatness. Yes, it was a prestigious mode of employment, particularly in a technological age that admires life-likeness.

But my heart wasn't in it. Ah, the heart, that delicate ...

Alas it is not that my *heart* is in doll-making either. I've discovered, strangely, that I never have had to engage the heart; life has come simply to me, including life's pleasures and pains. I've never been much for thinking or feeling, nor had a need to distance myself from either behavior. That is why my wooden dolls are so pleasing. Expressionless—you could even say wooden—they mean nothing to anyone except to the children who love them. I find the one-to-one relationship of thing to meaning extremely . . . pleasant. Indeed, pleasant. Relieving.

Here at Triple E, I find myself in communion with nature. I gather the wood in the forest and sit in my little back room. Wearing fingerless mittens, I make the dolls. Or rather, the dolls instruct me how to make them: I can't say I'm glad about this, but I hear the wood talking. Or maybe it is the trees.

In the end I had no pride in my profession as a Figurist. Strangely, for people often tried then to ply me with drinks and invite me to parties—and bed me! Yet I found that if I attended for drinking or love-making, they expected me to give them something—to gush over their portfolios or scripts or paintings—and goodness, I never knew quite what to say. "You don't understand," I wanted to tell them. "For me figure-making is simply a natural skill. I have nothing to *say* on the subject of what you yourself create." Oh, not out of hostility toward their sweet needs! Just lack of interest, you see. So of course it was not the profession for me—so public. Besides, filling things out with *expressions I myself had to design*, that wasn't for me. What a strange new tradition it seemed—so limiting and so very human.

When I was a child, the world seemed so lifelike to me. Uncanny! Ha! Hee!

chapter thirteen

TWO SISTERS

W here are you going?"
    "To town."
"You to Waban, me to Waban. Wonderful, excellent,
let us be going."
    "Are you still married?"
    "Alone again."
    "You alone, me alone, you to Waban, me to Waban.
Wonderful, excellent, let us be going."
    "Do you have children?"
    "They are imagined."
    "Children imagined. I am alone, you are alone. You to
Waban, me to Waban. Wonderful, excellent, let us be going."
    "Have you seen our sister? What is she doing?"
    "She always is sewing."
    "Our sister is sewing. Wonderful, excellent, let us be
going."
    "What sort of dolls are you making?"
    "Knock-kneed, pigeon-toed, lame."
    "Oh, how darling! And strange."

"Dolls"

chapter fourteen

It would not seem at first glance that I am suited to this sort of employment, which requires only physical labor. In the past I worked in the most computerized environment you ever have seen. I found it so pleasing. To work every day in uniform—self-prescribed, of course, as our department was called "Creative" and others liked to express what they perceived as themselves—well, a uniform was easy for me. I always wore a black pencil skirt, white blouse, and black pumps to stand at my "drawing." There I moved my fingers over the board and watched as the images flowed. I did not have to lift even a pencil or pen. All I had to do was think an image and color it in with my mind, and there on the glowing screen it would appear.

Despite my uniform, I was considered airy-fairy, thought to live on the shiny surface of things. This is not an incorrect judgment of me. And indeed, it made me seem an odd match for becoming what is known as an "artist."

Creative. Artist. The terms are bad enough, let alone together—creative artist! Ugh. I do not see that these terms describe what the people they're applied to even *do*, to be honest. I've never begrudged anyone their own self-opinion, however; if anyone wants to see what they do as artistic, so be it.

An absence of depth has always pleased me, however.

Regardless, I did love my position at the studio, despite the assumption I am a Creative. With technology I could conjure anything right there on the monitor's screen—oh it was lovely to feel just like a beautiful robot! The only troubling thing was how people (producers, actors, critics, not to mention every-day citizens) thought there was magic at work.

It was unfortunate when I lost my job, or relinquished it, but what was more unfortunate was realizing so late in my life the real dread of human existence. Until that time I was happy indeed. I can't argue with the studio, which became disgruntled when the pencil skirts and tidy blouses and pumps of their top animator gave way to hair in which literally nested some baby mice (dear mice, it was not my right to kick them out into the cruelty of the human-made city!)—and whose clothing resembled Cinderella's long, long, long before she was transformed. Blessed brown sacks, worn satin slippers. My dear ragged friends.

Yes, yes, it is true: this was around the time I began to read fairy tales in the evening. As I watched the smog come over the city and a Technicolor sunset brighten the filthy sky, I would read about girls dressed in donkey- and cat-skins. What was the difference between the animals and us? Nothing. How could I wave my arms over a table and conjure unicorns and dragons in animation, for people to buy and consume?

Better to live in the real dirt of existence. Its beauty. Now that is a fairy tale. When people reject this, it can only lead to sadness or anger, as it did with my sisters.

Now my hands have to do everything—gather eggs, deadhead flowers, and whittle at branches until faces appear. Yet in some very significant ways the work is not really so different; or I am not different, it seems. I am an automaton in the making of things. I do not imagine. I think.

chapter fifteen

THE LADIES' ROOM

When I worked at the studio I was considered a woman exceptionally skilled with stories of magic. Deeply admired for my dexterity with the uncanny, I also was praised for my intuitive logic. My position was very high: I decided on all the colors for movies.

One of my underlings—or so she liked to be called—held rational views, and often expressed the conviction that ghosts simply did not exist. It was a bit of an obsession of hers. The films we were charged to illustrate with animations were always about spirits—fairies, godmothers, ghosts. These were obvious fictions, not real life, she would argue.

I greatly liked the underling, though I knew that her views were foolish. Ever since I was a child I have believed in the fairies—and it has brought me great joy.

One day, the underling had an unexpected visitor at her desk. The woman who appeared wore black clothes with white lapels. She was very small—less than five feet—and had a gleaming cap of hair on her head that seemed to change colors in the fluorescent light. I joined them—it was time for a break in any case, as I had reached the end of usefulness on a particular task—and the conversation touched on many arcane subjects that did not make obvious sense (pomegranates, chariots, fields).

Eventually the subject at hand turned to ghosts, and my underling and the stranger obviously held strong and contradictory opinions. They argued for a long time, unhappily, while I stood there shifting this way and that in my black pumps, smiling upon both women as was my style; I was known for my smile, how it shone with rare attention, yet was not contrived.

And eventually, I put an end to their bickers. I purported that we were under a deadline and that the underling needed to turn to the main character's dress immediately, without argument. The dress was supposed to be robin's egg blue but, when enlarged on the screen, was showing up as puce for some reason. I did not want the stranger to feel unwelcome, so I invited her to contribute opinions. Besides, I concluded, I considered both the stranger and the underling to be bested by the obvious fact, which was that ghosts could not be proven to exist, or not to exist., and that we could all hold to our convictions, correctly or not.

That way, I concluded, everyone could be happy!

The stranger, who, if I have not yet mentioned it, was very attractive, said, "Lucy, you are more than clever with words." She continued in a surprising, dark tone: "But, your reasoning is not golden to me. For I myself am a ghost and I have been assigned to take you. Your time expires tomorrow."

There was a brief pause, and then the underling said, "That seems sort of blunt."

I myself was not surprised. My sisters had been taken to darkness many years ago, one after the other. So far I had escaped—I thought it was simply my nature. Like in a folk tale: my luck. But maybe there was some sort of curse upon the whole family, or at least upon its girls. Perhaps because we were Jewish. This all occurred to me too quickly and without any logic; looking back I know I was in a state of unconditional panic.

Yet the underling, who was rather fond of me and often did errands for me without my even asking—dry cleaning, shined shoes, and the like—pleaded in distress. Finally the ghost said to her, "Do you know anyone who resembles Lucy?"

"Yes," the underling said. "Both of her sisters."

They both slowly and creepily smiled.

Then the ghost and the underling disappeared into the ladies' room for a while, exchanging conspiratorial glances. They walked there arm in arm. How they had suddenly become compatriots I did not understand, but it too did not surprise me. Some women are inclined to join forces and gang up on other women. Everyone knows this.

When they emerged from the ladies' room they each held one knitting needle, which they carefully placed at my temples. Then they began, with their palms, to tap them right into my brain.

"I feel some pain in my head," I said. "Just a slight . . . yes, there . . . oh, if only you hadn't insisted on my calling you *underling*," I said to my assistant. "So hierarchical, so . . ." and then I felt something sublime.

Of course, I have no memory of the incident to this

very day, apart from a sentimental relationship to computerized animation—despite the fact that, now deceased, I live in the forest without even a TV or phone.

chapter sixteen

The four Gold children were up in the attic at their grandparents' house. Covered in dust, the attic was musty and hot. Its pale flowered wallpaper peeled; its floorboards creaked; dead spiders littered the corners. Lucy sat and read in the room with the sloped ceiling, where poor, slow Aunt Gimpel had slept on a cot.

The book Lucy was reading featured a resilient heroine. Either her nickname or her father-figure was "Daddy Long Legs"—it was unclear to Lucy which was the case. Perhaps she had long legs, or the father-figure was actually her uncle? Lucy adored the faded blue cover and line drawings inside and had read it many times up in the attic, beneath poor, slow Aunt Gimpel's bed.

What enraptured Lucy about this novel was the fact that the girl was an orphan and was sent off to boarding school. There she had the great fortune to wear a uniform, make friends, and learn how to dance.

(The book's font, Garamond, was also hypnotic for her.)

In the other room, with its unfinished walls and one dirty window, Merry, Ketzia, and the brother played dress-up. Lucy gazed through the doorway and watched as Ketzia reluctantly pulled cracked leather boots over bare feet. Merry had her arms crossed and stared at Ketzia with a strange expression set on her face. The brother peacefully sorted through magazines nearby—Merry had told him to look inside them for girls who looked just like her (brown curls, long limbs, hazel eyes).

Light from the window was spectacular—so yellow, so soft.

Lucy's brother ran over to her. He whispered, "They're all naked!" Together they laughed. Oh goodness!

Lucy turned back to her book about the girl and the kindly man who paid her way at boarding school. Like the girl in another book, the one who became a ballerina in London, this heroine was *deserving*. Also like the girl in another book who became a mystery writer, the one who ate apples up in an attic. And the girl who found her father after the war, and once, before she found him, an Indian servant gave her a monkey! And the girl who carried her sisters all in a basket, after a bad man had chopped off various parts—she ended up queen.

You were born into goodness, Lucy knew. Goodness was not something you could design or desire; goodness just came with you (or not), though you had to remain calm or it would depart you. Like happiness too.

Lucy thought to herself, "Life is magic that way. Wear blouses, oxfords, and skirts. Take ballet . . . have an interest in flowers . . . approach long-legged men . . ." She ticked off the motifs that frequently accompanied the Deserving in books.

Downstairs the Gold children's parents and grandparents prepared lunch. And just like that girl in the book who read in an attic—Lucy too read in an attic! Life was wonderful already—wasn't it? Life was a dream. Life was a book! A book skipping along a path strewn with roses and hung with garlands—the volumes all in a neat row. Skipping happily down the worn path, the beautiful path lit with sunlight!

In the other room, Ketzia quietly wept as she stood at the window, bathed in pee-yellow light. Undressed except for the boots. Merry, idly twirling her hair, considered the scene.

"No," she said. "That's not right at all, Ketzia. Stand just on one foot, with the other foot up at your knee, turned to the side. I don't care if it makes you dizzy—if you fall down, that's your problem, loser."

From poor Aunt Gimpel's quarters—pink roses on the walls and on the curtains—Lucy could not hear them. She was too busy imagining herself in a book being written that very moment by a wonderfully kind and intelligent person.

chapter seventeen

CLEVER LUCY AND
FOOLISH KETZIA AND MERRY

M y mother had three daughters and one was Ketzia the cuckoo. Ketzia was hospitalized early on in her days, leaving me home with Merry, who always ignored me. Except when Ketzia was home—then Merry showered me with affection just to make Ketzia feel bad.

Of course my mother liked me the best because I was easy. Ketzia was difficult, very needy; and Merry was mean, very unpleasing. As for me, Lucy? I agreed to any clothes our mother picked out at the mall, and wore the same shade of lipstick as her.

How I loved coming home after school! It was the most wonderful feeling. I sat at the kitchen counter, my chin cupped in my palms. My mother would make me a ham and cheese sandwich with mayo and I'd carry it into the den, where very often, my mother vacuumed while I watched TV. Unlike Ketzia, who became annoyed by the sound, or Merry who disappeared to her room or out with a boy, I would sit on the couch with my knees folded under my skirt, and joyously watch as the vacuum went back and went forth, nibbling now and then on the sandwich.

After the cleaning, often there was nail polish or cooking to do. Clear nail polish, of course—vanity is never a virtue. Clear polish protected the nails for the housework, and added just a hint of shine. It was very clean! Like the kitchen!

It was curious to me that my sisters had such immense emotional problems. Those are difficult for me to imagine. What could possibly cause such desperation in a very good home?

Unlike my sisters, I enjoyed school—though I knew the other girls, including Merry, were often quite mean. This simply did not affect me. I learned quickly that if one did not show any weakness, the girls would avert their meanness, direct it elsewhere (usually toward my class's version of Ketzia). Such an easy lesson to take away from the very first day of middle school; it is difficult for me to imagine a person not fathoming this.

And I could not claim ethical responsibility for the girls who were bullying Ketzia, for they would have bullied her whether or not they also could bully me, and there was no stopping their nastiness. Some girls will always be mean. One must rise above it in spirit, you see.

Merry, one of the mean ones, may have had her own social problems but you never would know, looking at her—no, her problems were more of a secretive sort. She was cloaked, inscrutable, and dangerous; you never could get an answer from her. Ketzia would blush and would cry and would cower. Merry would stare.

Different people have different problems, unless they are problem-free.

Did I have troubles? No! I was happy! Happy happy happy!

Every day when I woke up I felt a rush of glee. I would open my curtains and look out at the street. There, robins would gather and blue jays and crows. Sometimes they stopped on my sill. The baby birds loved my windowsill especially and would sit there with their light fluffy feathers just staring at me. I would pat the air in my bedroom, looking at them, pretending to pat them. Darling birdies!

On the summer lawn, often I could spy a sweet and grey rabbit. From the woods in every season I could hear the murmurs of people who walked in the morning—I found these sounds comforting, the sounds of a town rising and waking. And the oak trees and maples would spread their leaves protectively over the dead-end of our street and shade it kindly—ours was a marvelous scene to behold and how lucky I felt to be part of this blessed existence.

From our house I could even have walked to the streetcar and ridden it downtown. But I chose not to go there.

Unlike Ketzia, who would ride the streetcar and come home with more holes in her ears, or new green streaks in her hair, and with the smell of clove cigarettes and coffee and wine on her body and in her garments, I had no reason to sully myself or reveal weakness of character through physical change.

And unlike Merry, who would sneak into the woods with vodka and boys, I felt my body to be like a crystal—a sparkling rock someone found on the ground and kept always tucked inside a tiny pocket, as a sort of totem or charm—no wandering into the woods, that was not for Lucy the Crystal!

All I can say is I felt so happy when my mother would come home from the market with those brown paper bags, brimming with riches. Pistachios that turned your fingers bright pink! Popcorn that rose in a tin foil dome! And all that was required of me? To make my bed in the morning, to attend classes and pass? To play catch with my father in evenings, to carefully work with him on my math? WHAT FORTUNE.

With my mother and father I felt profound safety.

Yes, of course I knew that around the corner of life something else waited—I didn't know what, but I did not fear it. I didn't want to leave home someday, but I would have to. Surely it would be marvelous and beautiful and amazing and real—whatever it was, it waited for me, it grew just as I grew, it was my other life, it was my future, and as I stared down the street from my window each morning and looked into the woods, I sensed my future waiting for me.

The biggest sin was that of my sisters—practicing their sorrow and hate.

Sometimes, while they slept, I would hold my hands over their bodies and brains. I tried to take the darkness from them.

chapter eighteen

It was evening. The dead-end was shadowed. Oaks and maples quieted down for the night; how peaceful it was in the summer evenings when the leaves slightly drooped, thirsty from a long day in the heat. If their white undersides blew in a breeze, rain would come . . . Lucy rested her chin gently in her clasped hands, elbows on the white countertop. Perched on a stool, she crossed her ankles in a prim pose, tilted her head to the right—just a bit—and turned up her lips in a pleasing but not overpowering expression.

Mrs Gold handed her a blue Pyrex dish and a package of meat. "Just take it out of the package and put it in there," she instructed.

"Wait, wait," Mr Gold said, bounding toward Lucy with an eager smile and laughing eyes. He scooped some of the ground meat with a teaspoon and put it into a tiny cardboard cup printed with mushrooms and elves. Heavily sprinkling it with garlic salt, he grinned.

"A little aperitif," he said, wandering back to the den where a baseball game was on and Lucy's brother sat avidly watching.

Evening . . . everyone home . . . everyone happy.

Leaves blowing in the warm wind.

The older sisters were down in the basement, but Lucy chose not to join them. It was dank down there—the cement floor covered only in a thin and worn carpet with mysterious stains. The pinball game with women that moaned was not an attraction to her. The ladybug and seal toys had been Merry's and Ketzia's—not Lucy's— and though for the dear riders she had great affection, she knew the sisters did not like her to touch them, even though they were too old to say so.

Once, Lucy had dragged the ladybug and seal up to her room. This was when she was much younger—nine years old or the like—and she hadn't wanted them to be lonely. One afternoon when she was down in the basement to help Mrs Gold with the ironing (television perched on the ironing board, turned to a talk show), she would pat the animal-riders and feel they were damp. This would not do at all, she thought, and Merry and Ketzia would not want them to mildew! So she had taken them up.

Little did she know how that would offend—especially Merry whose eyes flashed with furious anger. Lucy never minded a correction, however; she took them back down the basement with care.

Down the basement this evening Merry and Ketzia played; Lucy could hear Merry's laughing. Soon Merry came up, bounded up the stairs two at a time, Lucy could tell just by counting. Bursting into the kitchen she grabbed Lucy off of the stool, spun her around, and sang her a song.

The spades go two lips together, tie them forever, bring back my love to me! What is the me-ee-eaning (clap clap) of all these flow-ow-owers (clap clap) they tell the stor-or-ory (clap clap) the story of LOVE! From me to you!

Lucy turned to Ketzia, when she came up, with a smile. But Ketzia was crying. Glazed with happiness, Lucy, of course, did not notice.

Suppertime! Mrs Gold yelled, though they were already all in the kitchen.

chapter nineteen

LUCY'S BALLAD

Miss Lucy had two sisters
The sisters had two bells
One sister went to heaven
And the other went to

Hello operator
Please get me number nine
And if you disconnect me
I'll kick your fat

Behind the Frigerator
There was a piece of glass
Miss Lucy sat upon it
And broke her big fat

Ask me no more questions
Tell me no more lies
The boys are in the bathroom
And they're pulling down their

Flies are in the meadow
The bees are in the park
Miss Lucy and her brother
Are kissing in the

D-a-r-k
D-a-r-k
D-a-r-k
Dark dark dark!

chapter twenty

THE MESSENGER OF DEATH

Long ago, I saw my own ghost, and it was then I decided to leave the city and all things that were human.

The city had been truly pleasing. It was magical and grave. The lights in the night twinkling, the people gathering, the buildings striving up toward the sky—striving toward heaven, I think. I understand that this has not been entirely disproved, at least to this date.

And the rolling hills, where I lived, I truly did love. Coyotes, roadrunners, and lizards lived there—animals I translated at work into pictures—it was comforting to be surrounded by the real creatures I was asked to approximate for children on screens.

It honestly never occurred to me to be unhappy.

I had been made Director of The Verisimilitude Department, you see. For many children, I was responsible for their only extended experience of "nature." How proud I was of this. As a child, I had lived on a street with deers and foxes, and the occasional hedgehog, but I knew how rare and blessed my own family had been.

Early one morning, I was walking down the winding road to my office, when suddenly a stranger appeared before me and cried out, "Stop! Not another step!"

This was not unusual in my neighborhood, which was very eccentric. The stranger wore a black Chinese robe and was drinking a cup of steaming hot coffee. Her hair was piled high on her head—her hair was white-gold, I want to call it. It sparkled, now that was strange . . . her hair coiled up toward the sky like in a Magic Movie production or children's book. Yes, looking back, I recall now that she seemed not-quite-real, even to me, who believed in the fairies.

"May I help you?" I asked her politely. As usual I wore my black pumps and a black pencil skirt and white shirt. My hair was pulled back in a bun and the only adornment upon my face was some deep red lipstick, just like my mother's. Next to the stranger I felt prim—and come to think of it, I always was prim, even when I was a child! Isn't that sweet? I liked to wash my hula-hoop nightly, and my dolls' hair . . . it was so relaxing to keep things hygienic.

"My dear girl," the stranger said, stretching a long arm toward me from out of her black Chinese robe. "You cannot resist me."

"No," I said. "I cannot resist any beautiful stranger. Aren't all strangers beautiful—don't you think?"

I was not sure what she wanted, but again, it was not unusual in the Hills (or anywhere) to encounter very confused women. She sat by the edge of the road and began to caress the dry grass that grew there.

"Oh dear," she said. She sipped her coffee. Just then a cup of coffee appeared in my hand—right when I wished that I had some.

"What will become of the world," she said, "if I remain lost? No one will die. The place will be so full of people there won't be any room to turn around in."

She went on like this for a while. "What will become of everyone," and so on. Not wanting to leave her alone, I turned my mind inside to my work. I had found, over the years, this was a pleasant solution when one didn't want to offend in conversation; simply think about something else while nodding politely! No need to ever express one's own ideas or opinions—especially if someone else seemed to want much more badly to speak her own. Much more fulfilling to avert the mind's gaze, and much more pleasing to the more-needy party, the sort of party who frequently appeared in my view, or so it seemed.

And I had much to consider that day. At work, I had been assigned a very difficult task. Impossible, really. An actor with a spectacular voice had been hired to play the leading role in a feature, and I was the one who would create her animatron figure. Yet the actor's physique was displeasing to the producers; they found her—how may I put this?—ugly. I was charged with paring and sculpting her likeness into a form they preferred. Yet I was required to do this without the actor ever knowing it had been done; somehow I had to make her think that she and her figure were accurately represented on screen. I had not yet come up with a method.

"Don't you know who I am?" the stranger was asking. She struggled to stand. I focused my vision.

Just then a young man jogged past us. He was singing a song ("Whistle while you work . . .") and his eyes darted this way and that. He glanced at me with pity as he went by, and then he leaned over and kissed the stranger. She looked, by the minute, more and more pale, as if she were disappearing into the background.

"The world is ending," she said. And then she truly was gone.

I arrived at work only a few minutes late. I booted up my giant computer—hard to call it a computer when its screens and knobs and armatures entirely filled the whole room—and I called to my assistant.

"Candi," I said. "Shall we make her dress black, instead of pink?"

"Oh, no, Lucy," Candi said. "We can't. I think."

"I'm just getting an image of black," I said. "And big, we have to make her quite big, yes, quite a bit bigger . . ."

I immersed myself in the clicking and dragging and filling in, and so the hours passed. Eventually I felt a tap on my shoulder. It was the stranger. She leaned in and kissed my cheek and the world went black. When I awoke I was in my house in the Hills. I lay in bed for a long time—days upon days. It is not so much that I felt unhappy—or mad—no, I really can't explain what had happened. I just couldn't move. I looked out the picture window and often some javelinas were gathered there, with their horse-heads on pig-bodies. Through the window, I heard them snorting. If the javelinas were not there, I gazed at the dirt.

Those were some of the happiest days of my little existence.

It was almost as if, in filling in the movies with animation, I had taken the life right out of myself—peacefully.

Soon after, I donated all my pumps, pencil skirts, blouses, and lipstick to charity. I flew three thousand miles inside a jet plane, and moved to the woods where I now make my home with the beavers, and bears. With the acorns and lichen. The mourning doves, some of our country's most common and humble creatures.

"With the Acorns"

"FRIENDLY ANIMALS"

Toad cries: "Hoo-hoo!" Child says: "Come on out." The toad comes out and the child asks about her little sister. "Have you seen Red-stockings?" Toad says: "No, not I. No more than you. Hoo-hoo, hoo-hoo, hoo-hoo."

LUCY'S SISTER COMES BACK

After Merry failed school and completed her time in the hospital, she came home for the holidays. By the time she arrived, the leaves had all fallen from the oaks and maples.

When we were children Ketzia always wept when the autumn leaves fell; and their falling made Merry angry. I became neither angry nor sad. The cycling seasons were simply marvelous to me. What a wonder that every year, the trees knew to let their leaves go—brown and dried, they would float to the ground. My mother and I would put on dungarees and cable-knit sweaters and rake them into the shrubbery beds. There, the leaves would feed the bushes till spring. Nature is beautiful, don't you think? I could go mad with my happiness for it, for the pleasure of childhood raking!

As we drove to the station to pick up Merry, I was excited. I had dressed up for the occasion in (yes) a pencil skirt, white blouse, and black pumps. I had gone to the salon that very morning and spent my last dime to have my hair done—straight as a pin, it was down my back in a blonde and flat pancake as was the fashion.

Because Merry was a designer—so talented she had already had a spread in the avant-garde French magazine *Mama*—the youngest dressmaker ever there featured—I had dressed up.

Yes, Merry had been tied down in a hospital, and not designing, for weeks; but she was coming back home so this was a huge celebration! One mustn't miss any opportunity for joy in a very short and minor existence.

I leapt toward the train as it pulled in to the station, and eagerly stood at the bottom of the stairs that, seemingly on their own like a mechanical animal, crept down. And she was first off the train, my oldest sister.

"Merry, what have you done?" came out of my mouth before I could stop it. Her hair was—how shall I put this? Her hair was so dirty and tall it looked like a nest. Yes, just as I myself favored! She wore what appeared to be prison garb—a grey flannel pair of pajamas, perhaps, sewn with huge and crooked stitches (white thread) into a sort of pencil skirt and blouse, but I could tell they were hospital garments.

As soon as I had spoken, however, I regretted myself. It is never a good idea to speak first, or to speak without thinking! To this day I will never forgive myself the infraction. I smothered my older sister with kisses but my error had been made and I could tell she was gone—her love for me was now absent and to the end I never saw it again.

"I was grazing horses—" she said with a vacant stare that went past me and then traveled through the heart of our mother.

Together we slowly walked toward my mother's convertible, where my father sat doing a puzzle. I spoke warmly to him. "Dad, have you finished it yet?"

"Nope," he answered. "Merry! What are you wearing?" He climbed out of the car and put her suitcase into the trunk.

At home, a great lunch was waiting: corned beef, tuna, and iceberg-lettuce salad.

"Uh," I said when we got home, wanting to think of the Perfect Thing to say so it all would be fine. Merry did not respond.

"Did you make that outfit yourself, Merry?" our brother asked her.

"The worms did it," she answered. "In the light of the moon."

I just wanted our family to be happy—my parents had arranged such a good and happy home! A fluorescent light dimmed on the ceiling; the kitchen's green walls faded in shadow. Outside the sky was blue, and acorns were dropping from trees: clink, clank, clunk. They fell onto the skylights.

Now Ketzia was nervously eating. My father was watching the Red Sox along with my brother. My mother had her back to us all, doing dishes, and Merry had disappeared to her room.

I stood there and smiled. "I'm just so happy we're all home . . ." I smoothed my hair on my shoulders and sat down. Carefully, I placed three olives and a slice of American cheese on my plate. But I could not eat. No— it was not proper for us to eat without Merry, who had been through so much, just like Ketzia—I leapt to my feet and bounded to the end of the stairway.

"Merry!" I called up. "Please, please come down . . . it's just not the same if you don't. We love you, Merry! We love you! We do! I love everyone! I LOVE YOU SO MUCH!"

I stood there and stood there, brimming and joyous.

chapter twenty-three

In our time," I read, "there was a little girl who set out to find the fairy tale, for she had heard everywhere that the fairy tale had been lost."

I had found this story in a grey book with a faux fur cover in the work library. We had a wonderful lending library at Magic Movies, and I found I always had it to myself. There was no one in charge of the library any longer, so no one minded when I ate my lunch at one of its old wooden tables. I must admit I had taken this book home without signing it out. The book just seemed so lonely in there.

Right inside its furry cover, this volume proclaimed to put forth radical views. "A radical glimpse into the history of fairy tales," the subtitle read precisely.

I had always been just this side of airy-fairy, just that side of logical. Hard to pin down my glazed state. It was as such that I had so excelled in my profession. No one expects a woman of mysterious humors to succeed at anything.

Somehow, in this particular moment, the book's advertisement of its own radicalism deeply appealed to me.

Perhaps this was due to isolation; more and more, even at Magic Movies I was the only person who seemed to believe in real fairy tales—just like the girl in the story! "In our time," that was a nice beginning.

To introduce her theories, the scholar narrated the brief tale about the girl and horse. In it, a little girl told her own story to an old horse, who listened avidly. She told him a story of another horse. *That* horse drank water by a stream and won many races. Yet still he was wild and lived in the open. The old horse listened to the girl's story of the other, race-winning horse. His old, foggy eyes glistened with happy tears. The little girl hugged him around the neck and then returned home. Around the dinner table with her family, she refused to eat supper: her mother had made some horse stew! Then the girl was accused of many unappealing qualities—by her own father!

In the evenings, after I came home from work, I was trying to adapt this tale to the screen. I had a computer program to assist me. I hardly needed my brain—only to produce the words and fill it all in! I was sure I could sell this one to Magic Movies. A girl who befriends a horse, and then refuses to eat him? This would be very popular, I felt, as we were entering an age of vegetarianism.

Yet popularity was not a value to me: I felt the story was both ethical and tender, and it contained magic. These are some of my favorite things, as you know.

The trick would be persuading Magic Movies that real fairy tales were acceptable stories to tell. Recently, fairy tales had been causing outrage among viewers; picket lines had formed. "Down with Fairy Tales!" "Magic Movies =

The Devil!" "Nature-Lovers are Fairies!" Two studies had received unusual attention on the national evening news: one that proposed reading fairy tales to children constituted a form of abuse; another that argued fairy tales caused women to be attracted to madmen.

Yet it had been my love of fairy tales that led me to this profession. They were my joy—my job to preserve them on screen.

I glanced at the clock. Far past midnight, I noticed; and I had to get up by dawn. I liked to get to work early. As the Director of Verisimilitude I found more than enough tasks to fill every day—and I was also trying to learn Chinese, Japanese, Vietnamese, and Korean, because new studios were cropping up all over the world. It would be crucial for Magic Movies that we create a working romance with our dear friends and neighbors!

The world was a very small place, getting smaller daily . . . but was also expanding! Wow!

After many attempts to write her screenplay, I gave up; my computer program always underlined everything I said as "poor sense." Or just crossed it out. Guess I was better off with color, not words. The trick would be to incorporate, through color, my message in the movies I already was assigned to be making.

You can see that with this new line of thinking—I had never been a "girl of ideas" in my youth—I began to succeed less well at Magic Movies. I stood by the water cooler all day trying to find fairy-tale followers. E v e n - tually, I depleted the library of its entire fairy-tale collection, taking every single book home. This, among other

71

infractions, led to my termination. It is without arrogance that I say when I left Magic Movies, so did enchantment. We went hand-in-hand, like a memory or dream.

At that very moment, too, enchantment left me.

"Hand-in-Hand, Like a Memory or Dream"

chapter twenty-four

MERRY AND LUCY

Once, for a brief time, Merry came to live in the woods with me. This was upstate, in a cold winter climate. Together we made ice wine—I had learned to ferment it myself in jelly jars. Sometimes, when we would boil the jars to sanitize them, Merry would get scalded. She almost looked happy when it happened. Yes, it is the only time I remember her looking happy—when she was burned.

From childhood she liked to self-harm.

I did not identify with this affliction though I never would judge it. As for Merry, she seemed to think that I did judge her.

"Why are you *yelling* at me with your *eyes?*" she would say.

Then I would ask her, in genuine curiosity, how it felt to be burned on her arm, and whether her body had feeling. Never any reply. I would turn to my cleaning with vigor.

Sometimes, it seemed Merry just wanted to get away from me, though I was the one providing her with the creature comforts of home. She would go outside and run into the snowbanks head-first—crash right into them with no worries about the ice that inside them formed in late winter. She looked like a mummy wrapped in so many clothes that she'd brought in a trunk. (I noticed, but did not comment, that it was a trunk of mine—or rather the one of our mother's I had kept at the end of my bed as a child.) She wore wool pants, knitted sweaters, rabbit caps. As she ran past me to sprint head-first into an icy snowbank, I caught a whiff of Old Spice.

"Where are you going, Merry?" I asked. It was freezing. Though I was enraptured by my life in the forest, I was not impervious to cold. Yet I could not resist still sometimes wearing my costume: my pencil skirt, white blouse, and pumps. Yes, this was a total indulgence, but in it I found great comfort and bliss.

As I stood with chattering teeth, wishing I could get back to my doll-making, Merry would run and run and run in the woods. Around a hemlock tree (somehow it had escaped death—and no hemlock ecologist yet had found it, though I wrote letter upon letter to them) she ran circles again and again.

"God!" she yelled. "I miss taking drugs!" She really seemed angry.

I ran toward her then, because she was my sister. "Merry, Merry," I said. "Come back in, and I'll make you supper. I'll make you tea. If you just let goodness into your heart . . ."

She threw herself onto the ground again in histrionics. She banged her fists into the snow. "Pills," she muttered. "Pills pills pills pills pills." There was a long silence.

"Vodka?" she said.

"I don't have any." This was a lie.

I stood there watching as she curled into a ball, and then she froze. Right before my eyes she turned into an icecube. It was *so small*.

Just when I was about to pick it up, maybe taste it— what would my sister taste like, I wondered, did someone mean taste better or worse than someone sad—she turned back to human. She neither moved nor spoke for a while.

"What's wrong, Merry?" I asked.

Finally, she spoke.

"I'm going to tell you something," she started. But I can't tell you what she next said. Fill it in, with the worst thing you could imagine: _____

_____.

"You don't know anything," she finished in the coldest voice I ever had heard or dreamed. "You don't know how to live."

I felt the beginning of horror coming along.

I never had made much of the fact that I had no memories after the age of seventeen. It was as if I had been asleep my whole life—enchanted, if you will. I had found it quite pleasing. Who wouldn't? Really, who needs all those happy memories? It would have been selfish to hoard them from people who have none—or worse.

But I had been wrong.

And I realized that the city-ghost had attempted to portent this moment to me . . . to portent this moment . . . shining on white horses they come with crosses and stars . . . my mind began to stumble. To make no sense.

Then a new light filled my vision. An empty light that badly transfixed me—I was staring into a disgusting, human-made sun.

I trudged through the snow in my pumps, gazing forward. The lame rabbit that lives in the trunk of the tree at the entrance to my cottage peeked out at me—poor little rabbit with just the three legs. For a moment, my heart lifted. I tickled her under the chin and gestured toward the hot, burning wood. She hobbled over to it, and then she sat down. I joined her staring into the flames.

Together we warmed.

I picked up some wood that I'd been carving for Merry; I thought if I made her a doll she could gaze into its face and see her own future. Children did that—why not my sister?

But I threw the wood onto the fire. Watched as it burned.

"I'm going to have to ask you to leave," I said to Merry when she returned. I did not ask her to leave to be cruel; read the next lines and you'll see.

After she left, I wept for three nights and three days. I dried my tears, and I died—leapt from the tallest tree into the air—and on from there.

chapter twenty-five

The street where the grandparents lived was leafy. Old and grand. A block from the streetcars, and next-door to a School for the Deaf and a Hassidic temple, the green Colonial with its black door comfortably sat; and as you approached from the car, you could smell the moth-balls from the front hallway closet. The fancy scent wafted from fur jackets (white sable, brown mink, and pink fox) right through the shut door to outside. Animals have a way of speaking to those who can hear them—even, or perhaps especially, when they are dead.

As Lucy entered the house, she would grab—per her grandma's suggestion—a penny or two from a bowl for good luck. The penny bowl always was full, and for people who came asking for help at the door.

How Lucy looked forward to Sunday visits. Deeply imagined them the night before, as when Santa was coming.

The dining room waited, already laid out with care. Pickles, green olives with red pimentos, sour tomatoes, tunafish salad made with two kinds of mayonnaise, and braided egg bread. In the oven was often a tongue, though

Lucy did not realize until adulthood that this was not just a food called "tongue" but was made of cow tongue. A cow's tongue roasting inside the oven, just sitting there waiting to be sliced up and eaten. How peculiar to realize tongue was tongue, Lucy marveled, to not have assumed it.

It was, in fact, Lucy's great gift that words did not connect with any particular, given meaning. To Lucy words were words:

Fiddle
Pennies
Movies
&
Tongue.

Words, for Lucy, were abstract, were pleasing.

Upstairs was a marvelous setting: a vanity table in the baby's room (as Grandma called it—it had belonged to Auntie Perfect) covered with tiny bottles of perfume, cigarette lighters, and old, dried out stamps.

When the games in the attic got too intense (Merry's eyes flashing, Ketzia's brimming with tears) Lucy would go to the baby's room and sit at the vanity table and smell the little glass bottles until their scent made her a tiny bit ill. In the beige room with its closet filled also with fur sewn in the shape of women's jackets, mainly rabbit, Lucy would then lie down. On the single bed was always dry cleaning, still in plastic bags, and she would lie on top of the cleaning and feel herself slipping, swooning from the perfume.

On the walls there were six framed pictures of ballerinas in poses. Lucy gazed upon them—imagining herself inside their tutus, dancing, bending, swooping like swans. Perfume and fur and dry cleaning and babies and swans.

Peacefully drifting, her stomach ever-so-slightly rumbling, Lucy waited for Sunday brunch to begin. Her mind was hazy and filled with sugarplum dreams. Outside the streetcar went by—*clang clang clang went the trolley, ding ding ding went the bells*—

That is all Lucy remembers.

chapter twenty-six

This job keeps me light in the mind, a state that I've always cherished. The workload is never too much, never too little, for me; one person can easily take care of the chickens and flowers in this small woodland setting. One wood-carver can easily keep pace with the dolls for the few children who visit.

Doll workers in factories don't often have this luxury. I have seen the same documentaries as anyone: all those women in white coats, like laboratory clinicians, sitting at giant machines, using metal pincers to deposit the eyes. The plastic dolls zooming fast on a belt.

In other doll-making positions, the speed is sometimes turned up in production, just as a test—we've all seen it in more than one documentary, have we not? Doll after doll head sliding past the technicians, going eyeball-less. Faster and faster, awaiting fulfillment that never does come. Over a loudspeaker, every so often, a reminder to love the country, and the jumping up of workers to sing for their leader, long dead.

I'll be the first to admit I felt a small bit of longing for just one of those jobs. Indeed I've always thrived on routine and that wonderfully rewarding brightness of spirit that comes along with employment. I used to work at one of the largest and most wealthy companies in the world and how I adored my routine—even the required uniform. Yes, hard to believe but the company required even its highest members to wear a uniform, though management called it a "costume." As for me, this pleased me: I was one of the only high-ups who insisted upon punching in when I arrived and when I left, just as I had when I was an intern.

I would have to say that despite the beauty of the forest and the talking to owls I get to do here, my job is now somewhat more difficult than my job in a corporation. All of this *freedom*. It gets to me. Airy by nature, I simply disintegrate, I think.

And (shudder) as a dollmaker in the woods, I am considered an *artist* by many. I do find this heavy, and I'll confide only in you that I also find it quite abhorrent.

For I have worked very hard in my life simply to, well, work! It is good for me and that is all I am doing. I take a piece of wood and I turn it into a doll. It's not very special, though I don't mind it at all.

It is not so different from what I did at the movie company amidst the smog and the machines; that was a little more abstract, as I approximated life with a computer. Yet I worked *very hard* to be sure that the word "creative" never once appeared in my job description.

The fresher air—the absence of fluorescence—I like that. But it comes with a cost. I can't pretend out here that the world isn't warming. And the economy: it presses upon the forest more than anything, really. World economics, all that. It's not exactly a refuge in here. But it is dark. That is the opposite of sad and of mean.

So.

I make wooden dolls and I love them.

The end.

chapter twenty-seven

THE DEATH OF LUCY

O nce my highest assistant and I went on a hike to the sign in the Hills. She was a good assistant, and accommodated my fanciful nature quite well. It may seem surprising to you that someone like me had risen to the top ranks of Magic Movies. It had happened in large part because ambitious young girls looked up to me and often threw themselves at me to pitch in to my projects. This could have been because I was so easy to get along with, and so happy, unlike many in the profession.

Also, I shared everything with my assistants—even film credits and what was known, in the industry, as *points.* That is money!

So if I invited an assistant to go on a hike with me, she always complied, and this was good fortune for me because I often was lonely. No, correction, I often was alone and only occasionally wanted company, but because my desire for companionship was so infrequent, when it hit me it hit me hard.

In fact, I had to be in quite an unusual condition to invite anyone to join me for anything, because I was so happy all by myself. If in my lifetime I ever have sought much company, I have few recollections—a handful. They'd fit in a matchbox.

We were walking up the rocky desert-like path above the city when, for no explicable reason, I was overcome by a desire to pick up a rock and put it into my mouth. There was a small rock on the path that reminded me somehow of . . . my happy childhood, or oddly, perhaps of a book? And so rather like when grown-ups say to a child *I could just eat you up* I had that irrepressible thought for the dear little rock at my feet.

This was unlike me—to have an irrational feeling—and so it was with great reluctance, I assure you, that I gave in, picked up the rock, and popped it into my mouth.

I turned it around, pushed it into a cheek, and felt the dirt wash off it and down my throat. But then the rock itself stuck in the throat, and I cried out to my assistant.

"Darling," I called out to her (I called all of my assistants darling), "Help! Help!"

But the words did not come—I called them out but had been rendered soundless.

A look of panic crossed my assistant's cute face.

"I don't have any water," she sputtered. Okay, so she had not brought any water, though it was the only requirement of my assistants on these hiking adventures. She started to jog down the path, presumably to get some from her car in the lot which was two miles away. But what could water do to help me, I wondered . . .

I could feel the rock still in my throat. Spreading a pink silk scarf on the path, I lay myself down just to rest, and thinking perhaps the rock would slide down as well, and deposit itself in my stomach.

Instead, I died.

So by the time my darling assistant returned, along with six other young women she had called on her cell phone in panic, I lay dead and did not move. Those poor young women; through the haze of death I watched as they all seven struggled to pick me up and carry me.

Everyone on the path joined them—movie stars, dogs—and as they carried me down the path I gazed up to the sky and thought, "Is this really the end?"

When I woke up, the doctors said that I had not been dead at all, and accused me of something *very* extreme, of trying to take my very own life! Apparently, in my bloodstream, they found a high volume of sleep medication. This would explain how I had to lie down, and some of the visions I had as I lay there—snakes hissing, bodies sliding into the ground—but I have always been happy, I tell you.

This was the beginning of a time in my life I do not like to remember at all. Everyone was concerned about me and I found that displeasing. Anyone, and especially "me," is the least important person of all. I am nobody, who are you, are you nobody too, etcetera and so on.

Eventually the psychological angle my life had taken really started to get the better of me.

And so to the forest I went.

The care
and training of your

PET
ROCK

"There was a Small Rock on the Path
that Reminded Me Somehow of My
Happy Childhood, or Oddly,
Perhaps, of a Book?"

chapter twenty-eight

THE BRIGHT SUN WILL BRING LUCY TO LIGHT

During my happy days as a figurist at Magic Movies, I would sometimes take my ideas to the company president, hoping they would catch his fancy. But it seemed he and the others in charge had little interest in princesses and witches. "Four quadrants," they'd say. "Hit the four quadrants." I didn't understand this at all, what it meant, and in jest I'd sort of punch the air with my fists: One! Two! Three! Four! POW! And then I'd nod my head in agreement.

Not much for math—none of the Gold girls had been, though Merry had always liked to count money—I shrugged. I guess I now see what they meant; to make money, story-products must appeal to the parties with money, and that's not usually a girl. A fact of our existence.

Over the years, it did seem that robots and oafs won out and the fairies just faded. Vampires, too, held appeal, but vampires have never interested me: they're so . . . fleshy.

Luckily I still loved what I did—always had—always will—and so I would leave those meetings never disheartened. I would go back down to my capacious studio, surrounded by my assistants, and get right back to work. Entering some numbers on a keyboard, I would watch a giant screen that took up a wall fill with color. For hours on end I would stare at a huge wall of one color and slowly tinker with it.

Over a long period of many years, the main responsibility I had—and it was a huge job in the context of film, even in an age when viewers could customize their own versions of movies—was to invent color palettes for entire productions.

What would look abstract to you, just a rose wall for example, to me represented millions of pin-point-size dots, each in a different hue, emanating a different balance of light.

One day, after making an unsuccessful pitch to the executives about a girl, a fairy, and a library threatened with closure ("Snore?" one of the men said loudly when my pitch started), I returned to my studio to find Ketzia there.

"Please," she said. "Spare me my life."

"Ketzia, what do you want?" I exclaimed. Often Ketzia made no sense. She was always so sad—how could her brain be expected to organize thoughts?

"You've got money," she said. "I don't want any of it, don't worry. But I think you can use it to help me . . ."

"I'll do anything to help you, my sister," I said, and wrapped my arms around her protectively. She was so frail, almost invisible. She was wearing an outfit of Merry's—little teeny mice made from real mouse fur lined her collar and cuffs and the hem of her skirt. Hardly surprising from one of my sisters.

As I stood there with my arms around her, for an instant that lasted a while, I was taken back to my childhood. And I remembered just how it felt there, that childhood full of children and often a chicken roasting in the oven, and the safety, the safety of that.

My mother who when I was young would rock me on a chair with red cushions that itched.

An Everflame in the fireplace. The refrigerator's kind hum.

I was surprised to find myself wavering on my feet. I righted myself and stood up a bit straighter. Ketzia was wavering too—had I sent her my thoughts? I have long feared I am reverse-telepathic. I take pride in my lack of neuroses, but that has been a quiet phobia of mine. It began in childhood, when my dolls began speaking *my very own name* after I sent it to them with my mind. I shook my head, clearing the path.

"The bright sun—I think it is too much for you, dear." I closed the shades of the studio but I was too late; Ketzia had fainted. This was no surprise as she could not have weighed more than one hundred, and she is taller than me.

Two years ago, she had lost everything—just like Merry. Ketzia her husband, Merry her job. Both of them possibly children. I don't know. Who knew? As far as I knew, Merry was living on the streets and was always drinking. As for Ketzia, no one had bothered to tell me she had been released from the institution, poor creature.

Two of my assistants helped me get her into my vehicle. I drove her to my apartment—I lived in a building that looked like a castle, where magicians had a cocktail lounge in the basement. I had lucked into it many years ago via a very secretive list. People were always inviting me to things; people always have liked me. And why not? I'm pretty and I am nice—not by design, but by nature. I set Ketzia up in the guest room, which was round, like a turret.

In the kitchen, I prepared a pot of strong coffee. I was about to pour some down my throat when the sun shone on the coffee, casting a reflection that shot into my eyes. "The sun is trying to help," I thought—it seemed the longer I lived in that city the more irrational I got, like my sisters. I did not like this. No, I decided it was okay—why couldn't the sun have its own inclinations? The sun was trying to help, the sun was trying to help!

At Ketzia's side, I knelt. "Dear sister," I whispered. "If you love me, please tell me what happened. Please bring it to light."

"I'm going to tell you something," she said dully. "So listen."

I'm terribly sorry, but I can't tell you what she said. You'll just have to imagine it here: _____ _____.

"But we—we were always so happy," I said, my voice breaking with anguish. My mother, my father, our house on the dead-end, the crows in the woods. The humming of summer evenings. The scent of skunk cabbage, all those beautiful, precious, miraculous things!

"This has nothing to do with them," Ketzia said.

"Did it happen to me?" I whispered to her then.

"Let me tell you another story, Lucy," Ketzia began.

"Once upon a time there were three sisters. One was mean, one was sad, and one was sunshine . . ." The story went on for a tremendously long time. I smoked a pack of cigarettes, called out for another to be delivered, smoked it, and drank several martinis while she narrated. And after the dark turn in the story, after the mean girl turned into ice, the sad girl to ruin, and the sunshine to bliss, the story came to a halt. Ketzia was asleep, lost in her dreams.

I was extremely unsettled. This story was worse than the other. Yet, when Ketzia woke up I pulled myself together for her. I made her some tea and buttered toast. She was in very good spirits!

When she could not overhear me, I called my father. I was relieved when he arrived just a few hours later by jet to take Ketzia back to the institution.

It was after they left that I entered the abyss.

Scientists believe now that the brain makes up its own stories based on its best guess of what has truly happened. My brain had invented beautiful stories for me, but then I found out they were fake ones.

Or were they?

The bright sun would not bring it to light, I discovered. The bright sun would not teach me anything. That bright sun was a liar. The sun was just a dead star. It was poison.

After that, my job did not provide me with much satisfaction. And so?

I died, and then I quit.

"ANECDOTE"

Once a turnip said: "I taste very good with honey." "Go along, you boaster," replied the honey. "I taste good without you."

Now dead, there never are days that I lose pleasure in eggs or in dolls or in flowers.

Carefully gathering the newly laid gems, I marvel at their dusky colors—subtle shades, mainly, of green, blue, and brown. And yes, sweet dolly faces shine up at me, from the forest floor, as I look for new little friends to design; all I need do is look for sticks just the right size and they speak. The perennial gardens need little tending— they offer themselves up in the most innocent fashion for human pleasure and that of the bees. Oh the bees; when I venture into the science these days, things look rather bleak—

But I cannot allow that to deter me from my peaceful path. Loss is everything, is it not, of our tiny moment on earth?

I'll be the first to admit that among my life's achievements, emotional depth would not appear. That is why it comes as such a surprise that I, among my sisters with their great anger and woe, would emerge as a true sprite of nature.

During my many years at Triple E, with so much time

to ponder amidst the leaves in the grass, I have come to understand why as a child, things were so easy for me—airy-fairy in my attentions, I was considered vapid, a bore, by my sisters. And who could blame them?

Yet in the larger and more competitive world, my superficial appearance did serve me well.

How I loved to live with my head in the clouds!

Besides, psychology is much overrated. No such thing is necessary for communion with animals or natural places.

To be a phony, however: now that's gold. One may float in real phoniness as on a rainbow or cloud. One may ride the heights of sheer bliss as on a unicorn or mouse-drawn carriage! If a mist fills the forest where one lives, and one is frightened by hoots or by hollers—all one has to do is sing. Evil begone.

I never have trouble at Triple E. Of eggs, dolls, and flowers I could speak every hour of every day and never get tired.

It is true that I dearly miss that old mode of enchantment—why, the books, of course, which I cannot bear to read. Sometimes I daydream about them—their ribbon page-markers, their pictures, their font. But, all it takes is a little slap on my cheek from a stern doll I myself have made just for this purpose—"Miss Brainless! Miss Bliss! Snap to it, you creep!"—and I no longer mourn.

chapter thirty-one

THE THREE SISTERS

For a long time, my sisters argued over which of them had more problems than the other. They argued and argued and neither would ever give in. Merry would be angry and cold and Ketzia would be sad and crying. And Ketzia always said over and over again that she just wanted everyone to get along—she who also would continue the arguments for hours, pleading her case! Merry sitting still, with that stony gaze.

For me and my brother, it was exhausting. I was always just happy, and so was he.

We leaned out of our bedroom windows one evening to talk. Our windows were on the corner of the house, beside the woods. I cranked open my screen and called out to him, and he cranked open his own and leaned his ear to the metal. We often did this.

"What's up?" he said.

"Not much," I answered.

We stared at the trees.

"Hey, so guess what?" I said. "Merry and Ketzia are in the hallway, and they're having some kind of contest!" I had saved this bit of news for him. I was a master of suspense!

We were both very excited of course, and crept into the hallway to watch. Our sisters were lying down on the orange and brown and black rug. Between them was a book called *The Joy of Streaking*. Neither was clothed.

After some hours, Ketzia rose quietly from where she was and ran toward the room where our parents slept, but she quickly ran back to her own room. As she passed us I could see that she was nervous and weeping.

My brother and I crept slowly toward our parents' room—not too fast, so as not to wake them—just to listen at the door and see if they were overhearing this mayhem. Oh, we were excited!

Just as we neared the bedroom door, however, we were overtaken by Merry. She passed us, naked, with such force that we were slightly alarmed.

I should not have been surprised when my brother picked me up in his arms at that moment and carried me back to my bed. I was the youngest, you see. Everyone loved me.

In my pink flannel nightgown, I slept. And he slept on the floor right beside me, in blue pajamas with feet. Is it any wonder that my mother loved to come wake us up in the morning? After all our sisters continued weeping and yelling over the intercom till then.

What a joy it was for me to fix coffee for her, and for my brother to pad out on the wet grass and retrieve the paper for Daddy.

chapter thirty-two

L ucy was a gorgeous child who, when she spoke, sounded to be singing a made-up nursery song, so gently and persuasively did she express her magic, and for this reason people were drawn to her "like bees to honey."

She was possibly the most *complete* girl who ever had lived, Mrs and Mr Gold both privately thought. Her lithe limbs and sparkling eyes and blonde waves of hair: she was like a drawing of a girl or a painting of a girl or a paper doll into whom life had been breathed by an angel.

Full, full, full of the wonder of being she was. And so easy from birth.

Lucy was not only easy for others, however. Lucy knew herself well, and this brought the whole world gently to her. She knew the very depth of her nature, and how it was totally shallow, and that this was good. What was missing in others was not missing from her. What was it, I wonder.

From an early age, Lucy enjoyed activities such as brushing her flaxen hair and painting her nails shell-sparkling pink and smoothing the coverlets on the doll beds. She enjoyed pretending to iron on the little pink ironing board made of metal; its pretend-iron even plugged in, always giving a wonderful touch of electricity to those littlest of hands. She adored kneeling at the bedroom window, hands clasped under chin, and watching the mailman deliver the mail, the milkman deliver the milk, the dry cleaner deliver the shirts. There was truly nothing Lucy didn't enjoy—and her enjoyment was not only innocent-seeming, it was innocent.

How exciting it was in the evenings, when Mr Gold would return Merry and Ketzia home from their lessons at the Academie Musicale. Her two older sisters, returned home to her again, the three graces reunited at last (every separation from her sisters and brother or mother or father pained Lucy—the only pain she truly knew was the pain of missing them).

On one such evening in winter, here came Merry, trudging up the snowy path, wearing a white rabbit coat bought from a mail-order catalogue, carrying a folder of mysterious songs Lucy loved to hear her play, and to which she would sing along ("Paperback Writer," "Cat's in the Cradle"). Here came Ketzia, sniffling, dragging behind, in the poncho Grandma had made her. Her brown, mousy curls stuffed into a wool hat from Daddy's office picnic last year: GOLD INC embroidered upon it.

Lucy put her hands to her cheeks, barely able to contain her pleasure at this joyous reunion. She pressed a hot cheek to the window and watched her breath puff out and make a cloud there. And then she kissed it.

O breath, o air, o childhood home, home of the heart and the soul and the being. Lucy had no words for this—

but she thought she was whole, and she thought that this was forever.

chapter thirty-three

I find that work at Triple E suits me well—the cycling seasons, the chores.

My sisters found that menial labor quite suited them too as they aged. Merry with her job at Triple C, sewing patterns for children's clothes, and Ketzia at Triple D, night-typing in the house of those bachelor detectives.

I am sure that our parents find it confusing that we three sisters who grew up in a town of such promise ended up in such, well, *domestic* positions. However, there are perfectly reasonable explanations for our lives of service: Merry and Ketzia are insane, you see.

It's a natural effect of having been tortured.

As a child it was as if watching two maniacs on the loose. Now, you would think that they were the ones who were under some spell, with their madness and nonsense. However, if you look closely, it is more that random acts of violence lit a match to their bodies and sent them spinning, like a firework snake.

Now that they have steady employment and permanent homes, it would seem that they have "come to their senses." But it is just the opposite! They were never enchanted. But *now* they are! Enchanted by *labor*—'tis labor has set them free.

If this is sounding complicated, forgive or forget it, please.

As for me? I had the most enchanted childhood, and never had much imagination. I was rewarded with money just for being, well, me. I never knew myself, nor wanted to know myself really. But one day, it is as if I awoke into darkness—yes, I woke up, though I never wanted to wake up.

I should say that I do love my job here at Triple E, gathering eggs and growing the flowers and gathering the wood and making the fires and tending to frogs.

It is strange, though. Always I considered my sisters to be imprisoned by magic, but it was me all along. Magic saved them, but it killed me.

Some days, I wish I never had been born, because then I never would have died—never would have missed such beauty on earth.

chapter thirty-four

SISTERS IN A PIT

I was on my way to town to sit on a bench and admire the birds, when I met a donkey. "Lucy, where are you going?" the donkey asked me. "To admire the birds," I answered with a sweet smile. It is always important to treat animals with kindness. "Take me with you," said the donkey, so I climbed on his back. The light came down through maples upon us. The donkey ambled down into the aqueduct that ran through town—below the houses and train. So we walked and came upon a rabbit. (There were still rabbits in those days.) "Lucy, Lucy, where are you going?" "To town, to watch the birds." So the rabbit joined us, perched on my lap. And then a squirrel, a chipmunk, a crow. At last we came to a ditch in the forest—we could hear the cars going past up on the street, this was no wilderness mind you—and the donkey jumped and fell into the ditch, and then I fell in, and after me the rabbit, and then the squirrel, the chipmunk, the crow. We sat there a long time. After a while, I became aware of a girl sitting near us. Slowly, I realized she was Merry. She had not yet seen me, and I watched as she dragged air from one cigarette into another, and lit its end. "F-ing a-holes,"

I heard her say. Looking the other way I saw Ketzia. She knelt in the dirt, her hands held in fists. "Why, why, why," she wept. I got all the animals with me to sing:

> *I'll be your candle on the water*
> *My love for you will always burn*
> *I know you're lost and drifting*
> *But the clouds are lifting*
> *Don't give up, you've got somewhere to turn . . .*

But they did not turn. They did not turn to me. I gazed at them a long while until finally, with the rabbit, the squirrel, the chipmunk, the crow, I got up and continued to town.

Of course, I left the donkey there in the ditch, for I knew that if I showed up in town riding on him I, like my sisters, would be considered insane. Which I wasn't.

chapter thirty-five

"THE GOLDEN KEY"

One winter's day, when the ground lay deep in snow, a poor boy was sent into the forest with a sled to bring back wood. After gathering the wood and loading it onto the sled, he was so cold that instead of going straight home, he thought he'd make a fire and warm himself a bit. He cleared a space, and as he was scraping away the snow, he found a golden key. "Where there's a key," he said to himself, "there's sure to be a lock." So he dug down into the ground and found an iron box. "There must be precious things in it," he thought. "If only the key fits!" At first he couldn't find a keyhole, but then at last he found one, though it was so small he could hardly see it. He tried the key and it fitted perfectly. He began to turn it—and now we'll have to wait until he turns it all the way and opens the lid. Then we'll know what marvels there were in the box.

chapter thirty-six

For the first twenty summers of Lucy's life, the Gold family rented the same kitchenette cabin at the seaside. A small white chalet with sky-blue shutters and what she remembered for many years to be a thatched roof (but was not a thatched roof) sat in a courtyard with four other identical cottages each with fantastic and mysterious names. *Clammer's Delight, Barnacle Billy's, Snail Castle.*

How Lucy loved to arrive that first Sunday at noon. Mrs Gold packed the children and suitcases and boxes of food into her VW bus (some of their neighbors whispered that they owned Hitler's invention—him being the man who killed Jews still to this very day, Lucy knew—how lucky they were to live far away from him and all evil!). The children ran in the aisle of their very own bus as it went down the Cape highway. They munched bologna sandwiches, potato chips, sucked root beer from straws.

Arriving at the kitchenette cottage, they made a great show of claiming their beds, though every summer they took the same ones: Merry and Ketzia in the knotty-pine room with sticky sap on the walls, Lucy and their brother down the hall in the windowless corner. Mom and Dad in the room they called The Bed Room for it was filled wall-to-wall with a mattress!

On the concrete patio, Mrs Gold set up the hibachi and the kids ambled down the street for fried clams to bring home for supper. They'd eat the fried clams while they waited for hot dogs and chicken wings to be done. After supper, as the sun set over the gravel parking lot, together they all walked to a glass booth at the edge of the driveway. Mrs Gold deposited coin after coin in the phone and breathlessly, overheated, the kids talked to their dear and beloved father, still at home because of his occupation.

O the chlorine, o the bats, o the daddy longlegs in the attic!

On Wednesday Dad would join them, bearing puzzles and bagels and soda and his fine fatherly arms to toss them, one after another, one after another again, in the turquoise swimming pool.

Waterlogged every evening, Lucy would sit on the porch on a towel (PEACE, MAN it said in rainbow letters) and dangle her arm over the edge of the wall. There, planted in row upon row, were Asian lilies, the purple, bell-like variety. If you took them between your two fingers and pushed, they made the sweetest *pop* you ever have heard. Lucy, an innocent darling, did not know that this killed the flowers.

That would have crushed her. Our child of wonder.

She wore a t-shirt with two fried eggs ironed onto its front. On a knee-scrape, one pink princess Band-Aid. Around her neck, a necklace of a green troll.

That sweet girl.

"Pop!"

chapter thirty-seven

Iwas a very good doll maker, I think. I knew when to
pare, when to nick, and what kind of cutting never to
use. Over-cutting, I think, ruins as many dolls as it does
actual girls, like my older sister. And, though I am now no
longer among the living, I used to be a marvelous person.
So listen when I say never to hurt yourself or another.

I fear there has been much slackening in the profession of being. Some of this is undoubtedly due to the
increased use of machines—though in my earlier days, I
adored technology to an extreme. Some of the degrada-
tion is of course due to the lower status of certain modes
of employment—sewing or typing—not to mention low
pay.

Difficult to say why so many who have so much are just
so despondent.

My final days at Triple E were a pleasure. Earlier, when
I worked in the giant city, each day was a hydroplane and
I the tightrope walker upon it. Oh, I appeared to be elat-
ed—built up by my riches (happy childhood, success in
the movies)—but the truth is, I never quite could fasten
my mind on anything for very long—except for the colors.

It seemed to others I preferred that. Most of my work at Magic Movies involved filling a massive wall with color, one pale, lucid, shimmering color at a time, until I reached just the right hue of expression. And so the color wall filled up my brain.

Yet there was a strangely unsteady feeling inside me, as if I was too contented perhaps?

I can't quite explain it, especially now that I'm dead.

I'll tell you one thing, however. I died by my own hand, by my own hand.

I knew it would ruin my parents, and I knew it would ruin my sisters, and I knew it would ruin my brother. But I did it, I did.

I had no choice in the matter.

The good news is, my sisters love their work at Triple C and at Triple D, and my brother will live out his days in a hard hat at the top of a skyscraper—the hat will, I hope, protect him from the sun's rays which beating down upon us are relentless in their beauty, the star is unspeakably lovely, it calls out our names one by one one by one one by one.

I'm getting away from myself. What I'd like to say is that you forgive me. Go say hello to a toad. Don't kill any spider.

Be strong.

chapter thirty-eight

FRIENDLY LUCY

When I was a child, I had a monkey-doll in a box at the end of my bed. "Hoo-hoo!" I said to the monkey. "Come on out." The monkey came out and I asked him if he'd seen my sisters. "Have you seen them? One has pink stockings, and so does the other." They'd gone to their music lessons and had not come home the same. The monkey said: "No, not I. No more than you. Hoo-hoo, hoo-hoo, hoo-hoo."

chapter thirty-nine

A RIDDLING TALE

For a long and spectacular time when I was younger, my sisters and I were turned into flowers. Our feet nestled in soil, our bodies covered up to our necks.

Our small mouths would open each morning and into them my mother would pour such fresh and wonderful drops of water. Right down the hatch! Right down the pie-hole!

Our mother loved us greatly and tended carefully to the weeds that tried to overtake our thin roots. Bitterly she would kneel at the edge of the berm and pull at them. Sometimes she was careless and disfigured a sister completely by error.

We were all gorgeously pink, my sisters and I. Some of our flowers emerged from the same root. *Inflorescence.* We had the most feathery petals. *Portulaca* among the wandering Jew.

One evening, I overheard my older sisters commiserate. "She thinks she's so pretty," one of them said to the other.

"She thinks she's better than us."

"She might be retarded."

"You have to be, if you are happy."

Before that, I had been basking in the warmth from the heated-up concrete of the sidewalk. And the love of my sisters.

But now a chill spread into me.

After a bone-numbing pause, in which several decisions were made which could not be reversed, I moved it from myself to my sisters. I shook it off.

Here is an important riddle for you.

Where do my sisters, my stories, now live?

And why am I the one who is dead?

Okay, that's two. My error.

Ha ha!

Rest in Peace
Lucy Gold

ILLUSTRATION CREDITS

Page 17   "Like This," "A monkey helping preen a donkey in
           the Galapagos Islands," C&GS Season's Report
           Wiles 1945, reprinted courtesy of the National
           Oceanic and Atmospheric Administration/
           Department of Commerce.

Page 25   "A House Full of Irrational Children," "Hop o' My
           Thumb" by Peter Newell

Page 38   "Dolls," courtesy of Ketzia Gold

Page 63   "With the Acorns," by crochet-pattern designer
           June Gilbank (www.planetjune.com), reprinted
           courtesy of the artist

Page 73   "Hand-in-Hand, Like a Memory or Dream,"
           courtesy of the Gold Family

Page 78   "Old Spice," courtesy of Mr. Gold

Page 88   "There was a small rock on the path," courtesy of
           Merry Gold

Page 109   "Pop!" courtesy of Florida Center for Instructional
           Technology, © 2009

Page 115   "Rest in Peace," courtesy of Gold Family

THE END